Volcano Escape

Owlkids Books

Chirp, Tweet, and Squawk loved to play in their playhouse. On this particular day, they were playing…

"Mountain climbers!" said Squawk.

"On the hardest climb of their lives!" said Tweet.

"Making their way up the rockiest mountain on the planet!" said Chirp.

"The first one to the top gets to plant the flag!" said Mountain Climber Tweet.

"Ready...set...go!" said Mountain Climber Chirp.

"I'm going to be first!" said Mountain Climber Squawk. "I'm going to plant the flag!"

Suddenly, the whole mountain rumbled and shook beneath their feet!

"What kind of mountain rumbles and shakes?" asked Squawk.

"The kind of mountain that is...*a volcano*!" said Chirp.

"And," added Tweet, "a volcano only rumbles and shakes when it's about to..."

"About to *what*?" yelled Squawk.

"About to erupt!" yelled Chirp.

"Run, you guys!" yelled Chirp. "Look out for falling rocks!"

"I'm looking for a faster way down!" yelled Squawk.

"Check in your backpack, Squawk!" said Tweet. "Look for something that could help us!"

"Right!" said Squawk. "I'll look in the box—I mean, backpack—with all the helpful stuff."

The three friends opened the lid and looked inside.

"I see popsicle sticks, a snorkel, and postcards from Chirp's grandma," said Squawk.

"Hey, there are also these springs!" said Tweet.

"Springs stretch really long, and then bounce back into shape," said Chirp.

"Like the spring in my pogo stick!" said Squawk.

"And that gives me an idea!" said Chirp.

Back at the volcano, mountain climbers Chirp, Tweet, and Squawk were planning their escape when...

"Look out for the giant rock!" said Tweet.

"Quick! Put the springs on your feet!" said Chirp.

"Look at me—I'm bouncing!" said Squawk.

"Boing-y! Boing-y! Boing-y!" said Tweet.

"Let's boing-y on out of here!" said Chirp.

"This is so much fun!" said Tweet.

"But the fun is about to come to an end," said Chirp, looking up.

"What! Why?" asked Squawk. "Why does the fun have to come to an end?"

"Because *hot lava* is flowing down the mountain!" said Chirp.

"Oh, no!" said Tweet. "The lava will destroy everything in its path!"

"Wait..." said Squawk. "Aren't *we* in its path?"

"We need to boing-y faster!" yelled Tweet.

"Boing-y this way, you guys!" yelled Chirp.

"Wait!" yelled Squawk. "I lost a spring!"

"Forget about the spring!" yelled Tweet. "Here comes the lava!"

"Hurry, Squawk!" yelled Chirp. "Boing-y over here!"

"But I can't boing-y that far on only one spring!" yelled Squawk.

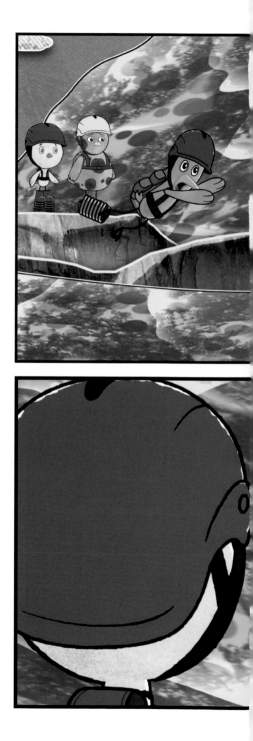

"You said springs can stretch, right?" asked Tweet.

"Right! We can stretch the springs to reach Squawk and pull him back here!" said Chirp.

"Let's make a string of springs to spring Squawk out!" said Tweet.

"Grab on!" said Tweet, as she tossed the springs to Squawk.

"Hang on!" said Chirp, as he helped pull Squawk to safety.

"Holding on!" said Squawk, as he flew through the air holding onto the springs.

"Thanks for rescuing me!" said Squawk, landing beside his friends.

"Time to boing-y on out of here!" said Tweet.

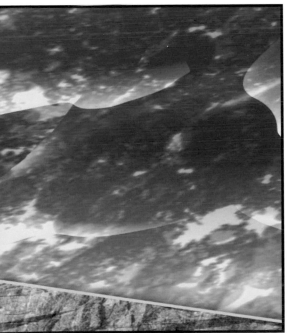

Mountain climbers Chirp, Tweet, and Squawk escaped the lava by bouncing the rest of the way down the volcano, singing as they went...

Boing-y, boing-y, boing-y!
Bounce, jump, bound!

Boing-y, boing-y, boing-y!
Rocks crashing to the ground!

Boing-y, boing-y, boing-y!
There's lava all around!

Boing-y, boing-y, boing-y!
We found a faster way down!

From an episode of the animated TV series *Chirp*, produced by Sinking Ship (Chirp) Productions. Based on the Chirp character created by Bob Kain.

Based on the TV episode *Volcano Escape* written by Bob Ardiel. Story adaptation written by J. Torres.

Owlkids Books acknowledges the financial support of the Canada Council for the Arts, the Ontario Arts Council, the Government of Canada through the Canada Book Fund (CBF) and the Government of Ontario through the Ontario Media Development Corporation's Book Initiative for our publishing activities.

Published in Canada by
Owlkids Books Inc.
10 Lower Spadina Avenue
Toronto, ON M5V 2Z2

Published in the United States by
Owlkids Books Inc.
1700 Fourth Street
Berkeley, CA 94710

Cataloguing data available from Library and Archives Canada.

ISBN 978-1-77147-189-3

Edited by: Jennifer Stokes
Designed by: Susan Sinclair

Canadä

ONTARIO ARTS COUNCIL
CONSEIL DES ARTS DE L'ONTARIO
an Ontario government agency
un organisme du gouvernement de l'Ontario

Canada Council
for the Arts

Conseil des Arts
du Canada

Manufactured in Shenzhen, China, in November 2016, by C&C Joint Printing Co.
Job #HQ3794

A   B   C   D   E   F

 Publisher of Chirp, chickaDEE and OWL
www.owlkidsbooks.com

Owlkids Books is a division of Bayard
CANADA